To:

Alison

ALOHA BEAR

**ALOHA BEAR™ AND THE MEANING OF ALOHA**
Copyright © 1987 Island Heritage Publishing
Tenth Printing—1990

Address orders and other ALOHA BEAR books and gifts to:
**ISLAND HERITAGE PUBLISHING**
*A division of The Madden Corporation*
99-880 Iwaena Street
Aiea, Hawaii 96701
(808) 487-7299

Printed in Hong Kong

# ALOHA BEAR
## AND THE MEANING OF
# ALOHA

Written and Illustrated
by Dick Adair

What is Aloha?
If you really want to know
Why everyone is saying it
Everywhere you go...

Then come with me
And we'll find out
Just what all
This fuss is about!

Aloha is "Good Morning"
And "Good Night" too,
"Hello" and "Goodbye"
And "I Love You."

But Aloha is more
Than greeting this way
More than just wishing yc[u]
"Have a nice day!"

Aloha means being there
In a time of need
With a helping hand
To do a good deed.

THAT WAS
A CLOSE ONE!

I scraped my knee
Got stung by a bee
This is more than
I can endure.

Then mom and sis
Apply a kiss
That's the Aloha cure.

There's a new little girl
Who lives down the street
She sits on a swing
Looking for someone to meet.

Let's make a parade
And march down to meet her
An Aloha parade
What could be neater?

Teachers and preachers
And all kinds of creatures
Are telling me what to do

It's a difficult task
To do what they ask
But that's Aloha too.

In a park or the zoo
You can ask any critter
The thing you don't do
And that is to litter.

When teacher is talking
And I've something to say
I wait till she's finished
To ask if I may.

You don't have to be literate
To be considerate
It comes from inside out
It's another way
To show today
What Aloha's all about.

It's not outrageous
Aloha's contagious
See? You've
caught it too!

But the greatest Aloha
You'll ever find
Is around your house
The Ohana Kind.

With family and friends
You're never alone
Surrounded with love
In an Aloha home.

After an Aloha day
It's Aloha good night
Sandman's coming
Turn out the light!

Gee, it's dark
But I don't care
I have Aloha love
and Aloha Bear.

Aloha's a spirit
Is what people say
Who live in this land
Of Hawaii Nei

It's more than a word
That much is true
It's our way of saying
We care about you.